STILL TALKING

STORIES

Still Talking: Stories © Estate of Lore Segal 2026
Introduction © Vivian Gornick 2026
This collection first published by Sort Of Books, 2026

Sort Of Books, PO Box 18678, London NW3 2FL
www.sortof.co.uk

Distributed by Profile Books
29 Cloth Fair, London EC1A 7JQ

No part of this book may be reproduced in any form without permission from the publisher except for the quotation of brief passages in reviews.

Typeset in Goudy Old Style and Mr Eaves to a design by Henry Iles

1 3 5 7 9 10 8 6 4 2

A catalogue record for this book is available
from the British Library
ISBN 978-1914502354

Printed and bound by CPI Group (UK) Ltd,
Croydon, CR0 4YY

GPSR details and contact
We make every effort to make sure our products are safe for the purpose for which they are intended. For more information see our website (www.sortof.co.uk) or contact our EU Authorised Representative:
EAS Project OU, Mustamäe tee 50, 10621, Tallinn, Estonia.
gpsr.requests@easproject.com

Still Talking

STORIES

LORE SEGAL

with an introduction by
VIVIAN GORNICK

Contents

Introduction by Vivian Gornick   7

The Half Century Dispute	15
No More Trains	23
The Forgetting Olympics	28
Funk	33
Death of the Water Bug	38
Left Shoulders	46
Why with an Exclamation	49
Next to Godliness	52
Beyond Imagining	57
Farah	65
Bessie	70
In the Mail	74
Grandmother Mole	78
Ilka	83
Who is Outside?	89

Publishing History   94

Introduction

Vivian Gornick

Lore Segal – not only a great writer but my good friend for more than twenty-five years – was famous for describing almost everything that entered her mind as "interesting." A dog squats in the street, a friendship begins to fail, a neighbor presses the wrong button in the elevator, a quarrel threatens between someone planting a flower and someone picking a flower, and Lore, inevitably, would say, "Isn't that interesting!"

Another of Lore's verbal gambits was beginning a sentence with "Why do you think it is that..." fill in the blank. Why do you think it is that people hate being corrected? Or being disagreed with? Or humiliated when a speaker at the table doesn't look at them? Or someone they've met doesn't remember meeting them? Often her stories were grounded in these or similar "Why do you think"s. The writing that emerged from such imaginative musing is one of the small glories of American literature.

⸺

Lore was born in Vienna in 1928, into a family of middle-class Jews. Nine months after Hitler took Austria, the rescue mission known as the Kindertransport was formed and arrangements were made to secure a place on it for Lore. She knew that it meant leaving her parents, perhaps forever, and, as she has written, that made her feel "as if my inside had been suddenly scooped away." At the same time, she reports, she was also thinking, "Wow! I'm going to England!" This was nourishing turmoil: a sinking heart coupled with an unquenchable curiosity. It became second nature to Lore and, in time, characteristic of the Lore persona – sometimes called Ilka, sometimes Bridget, sometimes Farah – responsible for the best in her novels and stories.

In the latter part of Lore's life one of her favorite forms of writing became the exercise in the short story known as flash fiction. In it she made brilliant use of a literary invention she came to call "The Ladies Lunch." The name refers to a group of very intelligent Upper West Side women (Lore and her friends) who'd been meeting for lunch every other month for some thirty-odd years, The ladies' agenda was whatever was on any one of their minds.

For Lore, the Ladies Lunch was writer's gold. It provided her with a setting and a group of models that allowed her to riff, in her remarkably original style, on friendship, aging, everyday obsessiveness, even useless philosophizing. In one of these pieces, the character called Farah confides that now that her vision is failing she listens to YouTube philosophizing that she doesn't understand; when Bridget asks what doesn't she understand, Farah replies "How does the inability of the finite to imagine the infinite prove the existence of God?"

A few years ago, Sort Of Books published some of these pieces in a collection called *Ladies' Lunch and Other Stories*. Now, in *Still Talking*, we find these delightful creatures gathered together once again, uttering new and even more magical Lore wisdom than the last time around.

A character called Lucinella tells the group that there was a time when she needed "to have my pencils in a row, sharpened to perfect points, all one length." After that, Ruth says of her friend Dario that often when he visited he would "sit and talk and fidget and look uncomfortable until he suddenly got up and straightened the picture on the opposite wall." And Hope observes that the nice woman who comes in once a week to clean doesn't put things back where they belong, and it's driving her crazy. The group is then made to consider: *Why* do Hope's things need to be in the right place? *Why* does Dario need to straighten the picture? *Why* do Lucinella's pencils need to be sharpened to perfect points? Various explanations are offered: because neatness is prized, because straight feels better than crooked, because you want to be able to find your things! "Yes, but why?" Bridget continues to ask. Why do I want, why do I need, why must I have.

In the story "Why with an Exclamation," Bridget has been rereading Proust. "The payoff," she said, "is that you come across improbable behaviors and recognize your friends – recognize yourself." For example, she notes that Proust has a character not give a friend what the friend wants. "But *why* do we do that?" Bessie wants to know. "This is not the 'why' that expects a 'because,'" Bridget replies. "It's the 'Why, how curious' with an exclamation mark!"

INTRODUCTION

The women are now in their eighties and nineties, and there's no question, aging is the condition at the heart of all their musings, a development that has not made them any less interesting than at any other stage of their lives. Bridget, Bessie, Ilka: they're as wise and colorful and distinctive as ever. They are, in fact, among the only people I know (real or otherwise) who have genuinely interesting – that is, enlightening – things to say, as a consequence of having grown old.

Bridget sees that aging has brought about a series of insecurities she's never before experienced; and, as usual, the new experience produces the Lore sentences that give the reader not the meaning but the *feel* of this new state of being. Ruth begs off a dinner invitation, then explains that she regrets having done that, not because she missed the dinner but because "it makes it easier to not go the next time."

Ilka says she's thought more than once "No more talking. There's something I want to say but my mouth doesn't open to say it." It's as though she "no longer had what it takes to make her way into the conversation."

When asked if she wants company, Bridget says "What I want is for this week to be the week after."

Everyone is forgetting names, words, occurrences, and someone suggests that they start the Great Ladies Forgetting Olympics. "You mean whoever forgets the most names gets the gold?"

Yet in the story "Death of the Water Bug," Bessie points out that "Insects are our Other." They "perfectly resemble us," she observes, in that they struggle desperately to not be stepped on because they too want "so immensely to not be dead."

These wisdoms do not exactly bring peace. In fact, declares Bridget in "Funk," "Anxiety is surprisingly uncomfortable. It's like not being able to imagine summer afternoons when your coat won't zip on a windy street corner in February."

Ah, yes, I hear Lore's readers murmuring to one another, I may or may not know what aging means, but I'm certain that this is exactly what it feels like.

Lore Segal was an original: one of a kind, we'll not see her like again soon. To the last day of her life she delighted in the feel of things: the sun on her face, a well-written sentence, the smile that begins on the mouth but does not reach the eyes; and then there was the lifelong amazement she felt about humanity itself. She often cried, "How curious human beings are!" That curiosity was at the heart of her talent; it is what made almost everyone who read her feel more alive in her presence, on the page or in person; more than alive: clarified. *Clarified*: one of the most beautiful words in the English language. I can see her nodding her equally beautiful head even as I write these words.

The Half Century Dispute

"I FORGET," Ilka says to the friends around the table, "do we allow ourselves to tell our dreams?"

"You have a good one?" Bessie asks her.

"You know the kind of movie in which something has to be prevented? In this dream, there is some fatal thing I need urgently to say to my cousin Frieda, but she is on the far side of an abyss, and then she is on the other side of a wall."

"What's the urgent thing you need to say to her?"

"The dream doesn't specify."

The friends, who have been meeting for lunch for some thirty years, live in a fifteen-block area between Riverside Drive and Broadway. They talk the politics you expect on the Upper West Side of New York, except when Ilka is talking to them about her cousin Frieda Fishgoppel, professor of philosophy, now emerita.

Ilka says, "The dream is something to do with our most recent reconciliation."

"Why reconcile when you know that you will keep quarrelling?" Farah asks.

"Our project," Ilka says, "is to be reconciled to quarrelling."

"But why do you keep the argument going?" asks Ruth, the bona fide retired activist. "You disagree with everything she stands for and disbelieve what she believes."

"And believe," Ilka says, "in her inalienable right to believe what I disagree with. It's in the nature, on my part certainly, of a demonstration, proof that we live in a democracy where people – and people we love – may have different, may have wrong opinions."

"And she is game to let you keep disagreeing?" asks Bridget.

"Nnnnno," Ilka says rather slowly. "But I like, I love, the intelligible, passionate language in which she disagrees. Frieda is in love with her truths in a way I do not love mine. And you all know that she was my ticket to America – my old ur-story."

"Tell it again," the friends say, and settle themselves on their chairs.

"AFTER THE END OF THE WAR," Ilka says, "Frieda searched for the western, Viennese branch of our family. The generation of the grandparents who weren't dead of old age had been killed in the camps, but there were cousins who had emigrated to Uruguay, to Paraguay, to the Dominican Republic, to Argentina. There is the uncle who went to Canada. Frieda sent the visa for me to come to New York. She settled me in her funny little apartment in Washington Heights – in the fifties, there were so many of us we called it Washingstein Heights. She handed me an Oxford English Dictionary and hurried back to New Haven for her exams. She would come in to see if I was O.K., bring me *David Copperfield* or a Jane Austen. I had arrived speaking minimal English, but all the refugees were soon reading novels in English, though maybe not the Henry James that Frieda brought me."

"What was her field?" Ruth asks.

"Frieda's first Ph.D. was in literature, and her dissertation was about antisemitism in her favorite writings from – I don't exactly remember – was it 'Beowulf' to Eliot?

"Frieda and I still e-mail. If we don't hear from each other, we worry. 'The earth is flat and has four sharp corners,' she writes me. 'It's easy to drop off the edge.' She has not replied to my last, and so I promptly assume that she has fallen! She is in emergency! Or, this time, did I go too far?"

"But what about?" Bridget asks.

"I'm trying to remember – what were we saying on the bus in Jerusalem," Ilka muses. "Frieda and I were travelling with a group of Americans – that was in the eighties. We were sitting, talking, and she remembers that I got up and walked away and that I got off the bus. I remember that we did not talk for the last leg of the trip. We didn't get together back in New York until Lotte invited both of us to dinner. She left us in a room together with the door shut, and Frieda and I started to laugh. You and I, we said to each other, we don't have to go on doing this. You know what I will say, and I know what you are going to answer. But to this day we are still arguing the same opposing politics without having made a dent in each other's opinion."

"Her wrong opinion, which leads her to vote on the wrong side," Ruth says.

"Which she believes to be the right side as fully as she believes that yours and mine is wrong."

"And you know the disastrous consequences of hers," Ruth says.

"That's why I walked off the bus, I suppose," says Ilka.

"But you go on talking."

"We go on talking."

Bridget says, "You keep not telling us what you argue about."

"Because I am more interested in the fact, the nature of disagreement," Ilka says. "Also, it keeps the conversation from going to Israel, though Frieda says, correctly I think, that 'to not go there' is to silence speech."

Ruth asks, "So exactly what is the dispute?"

Ilka says, "One way of putting it is that I choose to think of myself as a humanist, a child of Adam, where Frieda thinks of herself as a child of God-chosen Abraham. The DNA, as she says, will be the same.

"I search for what Isaac, the progenitor of Israel, has in common with his cousin Ishmael, progenitor of Canaan: they both laugh if you tickle them and bleed when you prick them, which drives poor Frieda frantic. She says Shakespeare probably never met a Jew in his life. She challenges – no, she demolishes – my dearest belief, that it's the imagination which could save the world, that if we imagined our neighbor's griefs we would not do to him what we don't want him to do to us. Frieda says that, having imagined what it's like to be the abused Jew, Shakespeare confiscates half his fortune, hounds him ignominiously off the stage, and makes him convert."

"I'm going to open a bottle of wine," Farah says. "Ilka, go on."

Ilka says, "Frieda argues that the basis for our innate difference is my inclination for seeing sameness where hers is for seeing distinctions. Where I search for harmony in equality, she sees how one thing – one people, history, ethos – is distinct from another. Frieda says that for me distinctions spell the disruption of harmony; that, for her, harmony is a lie where distinction is present.

"'Harmony?' I holler. 'What, me? Aren't I your favorite contrarian, your in-house skeptic who tests your every certainty by opposing my uncertainties? Do, please, notice,' I tell her, 'that I end with my universal question mark.'

"But then she asked if I and you – my 'Lunch Ladies' – still vote on the left and I said, 'You bet,' and we were back on the bus, you see. I e-mailed her: 'I'm discouraged.' She answered, 'For the record (if there is a record) I feel terrible, not simply discouraged but terrible.'

"I wrote her, 'I don't know if it will ease your distress, but I reconfirm my love and friendship if you will accept them with the acceptance also of our irreconcilable differences, which are totally unchanged after half a century's disputation.'

"She answered, 'Noted. Confirmed and renewed.'"

ILKA SAYS, "And then I dreamed that there was something essential that has to be prevented."

No More Trains

"No more trips, no more traveling," Hope said.

"Except to go and see Lotte at her 'facility,'" Ruth said.

It was early one September. The friends had taken the train to Old Rockingham to have Ladies' Lunch at Bessie's. Colin, who was having one of his bad days, had gone into his room. They lunched on the wooden deck overlooking the curling blue bay with its traffic of pleasure boats. "Like so many little white triangles. It's lovely," they said, and Hope added, "But no more trips."

"The Connecticut train out here wasn't bad," Ruth said, and Hope said, "Oh, I like the train. I always feel that little thrill as soon as I sit in the taxi to the train or to a plane. It's the anxiety of the days - of the week - before a trip that's hard to survive."

"Oh, that. Yes," they had all agreed, and Farah said, "My balance is shot, and, with my eyes getting worse by the day, it's the *thought* of the two blocks to Broadway that produces a small agoraphobia."

Bridget said, "I feel - do we agree - that we don't need more adventures, don't need new experiences? That we can batten on past travels?"

Bessie said, "The time Lotte and I and our two guys lit out for Europe after our final exams - the four of us lugging our bags, the only people out in the streets of midnight Venice."

"China," Bridget said. "In the eighties. We noticed the designs on the houses along the Burma Road - each village had its signature. A very old woman bent down to her grandchild and pointed at me: 'Look! An American.'"

Ilka said, "When you've made it up the mountain, you get to look over the top, and there is a new bit of the world that you could not have supposed."

They continued to meet for Ladies' Lunch and continued to say "If someone would drive us we could go to see Lotte in Green What's Its Name." Lotte had begun to call them, hallucinating missing keys to a car that she seemed to believe she had brought to take herself home to her apartment.

"We didn't - we couldn't go to see her," they said after Lotte died. This, too, is now - how long ago?

AT LUNCH IN NOVEMBER, Ruth said, "I accepted an invitation to dinner - another one of these longtime get-togethers - and at the last moment it seemed too complicated and I begged off."

"And you regret not going?"

"Not the dinner, and not the not getting together so much as not having gone, which makes it easier to not go the next time."

Bessie said, "Colin can no longer do without me, and it's getting harder for me to take the train into the city. I'm going to let Eve have the Ninety-fourth Street pied-à-terre. The light is good for her painting."

"No more lunches at the Café Provence," said Hope, who'd learned that her old friend Jack had died. "That was in June," she said. "Curious to have been living for months in a world without Jack living in it."

"So can we batten on the love it is better to have had and lost than never to have had at all?" said Bridget.

"Yes," Farah said. "Yes." And her friends waited for the story. Farah said, "I've been toying with a notion that losing my sight is the punishment for my great, grand forbidden affair."

"Oh, for goodness' sake, no you haven't! You don't really believe in punishment," Ruth said.

"I really don't," said Farah, "but punishment feels like the right idea."

"You mean that you wouldn't do it if you had it to do again?"

"Yes, I would!" said Farah.

"Will you tell us the story?"

"No," Farah said. "Did I mention that Medicare is sending me a walker?"

THEN THERE WAS COVID and their children worried about them. Ruth undertook to Zoom Ladies' Lunch. They became accustomed to watching themselves talking to one another out of squares that showed their beds, their bookshelves, the doors to their bathrooms. It turned out to be easier to stay at home – not to have to leave the house. Then, one day, Ruth e-mailed everybody to ask if anyone would mind if they took a hiatus. Nobody minded, and it has become easier to not have Ladies' Lunch. For now?

The Forgetting Olympics

FARAH SAID, "Ladies' Lunch at my place, my agenda: Forgetting as an Olympic sport. You know how TV uses competition to turn us on to baking, interior decorating, fashion, and what all? I propose the Great Ladies' Forgetting Olympics."

Bessie said, "You mean whoever forgets the most names gets the gold?"

"Forgets more words, words, words," said Bridget.

"And dates and appointments," Farah said.

Bessie said, "Addresses. I remember Lotte calling me several times for the address of the party that turned out to be - I forget, what do we call a Jewish wake? - for Sylvia's deceased aunt. Poor Lotte spent the evening trying to remember from where she knew Sylvia or if maybe she had never met her."

"Forgetting people," Ilka said. "I had an e-mail from a Samson who writes as if I should know his brother, his mother? The only Samsons I know are Kafka's bug and the one in the Bible."

"I picked up a story I published in 2007," Bridget said. "It's not that I don't recognize what I wrote, but I couldn't think how it ended."

"So anyway," said Farah impatiently. "This is this morning. I'm enjoying my coffee, going to turn on the news, and I think, Wait a minute - today is the fifth? Imagine yourself in an elevator in free fall, your stomach has been left behind, or drops into your boots - or is it your heart that drops into your pants - I forget the idiom, but wasn't it on the fourth I was having dinner with Ervin?

"Ervin's folks are my mother's distant cousins who went to Canada. Ervin is the in-between generation, younger than my son but older than my grandson Hami, I think. Anyway. So. I marched myself into my office, turned on the computer - I have this big desktop because of my bad eyes - got briefly hysterical when I couldn't remember how to find the calendar, found it, and it was! It was yesterday that

Ervin was in town. I see him sitting at a table waiting for me, except that I can't remember where we were supposed to meet..."

"Wait!" Ilka said, "Wait, wait, wait! Samson! Lotte's son was Sam and his brother Gregor came from Chicago, was it? And they put Lotte into... what's the name of the assisted-living place?"

Farah said, "I had to decently wait till nine o'clock before calling, and I reached him at the airport, already in line to board. It was a slow line. I said, 'Ervin! It's this sorry old head of mine. I forget things!' He said what we all routinely say – he says, 'So do I. I forget things, too!,' meaning, If *I* forget, forgetting is nothing to do with *your* embarrassing old age. 'I forget everything all the time!' he says. If he thinks he's going to out-forget me, he has another think coming. I say, '*I* forget names, words, and dates, and yesterday I forgot that it was the fourth.' So he says, 'And I can't remember the number of Cousin Hami's phone,' and we're off to the races. I say, '*I* can't remember my own phone number, and I forgot my keys inside my apartment and had to call the locksmith.' He says, 'I left my bag in the hotel room. They will have to send it on.'

"And now he's one up on me because I'm not going to tell him, I have forgotten *you* and what you look like. If we passed in the street I wouldn't know you.

"Ervin said, 'The line is beginning to move. Goodbye, Aunt Farah.' I said, 'Next time you're in New York, you'll come and have dinner at my place and I'll take you up to our roof and show you the Hudson River right underfoot.' 'You showed me already,' he said. 'You've never been in my place,' I said. 'Sure I have,' he said. 'Last year, when I was in town, and after dinner we took drinks up to your roof. Goodbye.'

"'Goodbye, Ervin,' I said. I try and try and fail to see Ervin sitting – on which chair? Facing in which direction? Looking over the wall on the roof? A mean trick if the loss of vision has taken away my visual memory."

Ruth said, "Like trying to force the raggedy tail end of a dream to reconstitute the dream before we forget what it was about."

Farah said, "Before we forget what there is to remember."

Funk

"Woke up in a state," Bridget e-mailed Ruth on the day of Ladies' Lunch. "I don't like to do this, but I'm not going to make it to your place."

"Do you want us to come to you?" Ruth e-mailed back.

"What I want is for this week to be the week after next," Bridget returned.

"Farah and I are coming over," Ruth wrote.

"I don't think I have any food," wrote Bridget.

"Hi! We've brought sushi," Ruth said, and Farah said, "Bessie and Ilka are on their way up. Hope might come a bit later. What's going on? Talk to us."

They seated themselves around Bridget's table. She said, "It's the stupid nerves *before* giving a talk.

I'm on this panel on Wednesday and I have to give the opening statement. This is stuff I do all the time."

"But public speaking is famously nerve-wracking," said Ruth, the retired lawyer. "I used to worry weeks ahead, and then only one week, and later one day, then just for the five minutes before going on, until I learned to just be nervous."

"And I'm frazzled by all the things I haven't got done around the house," Bridget said.

"Like what, for instance?"

"Like... I can't remember – and I don't know how to find – the name of the guy who washes my windows, so I can't call to find out when he is supposed to come. Hope, hello!" she greeted the latecomer. "Sit down. Have sushi."

"Sorry I'm late," Hope said. "What's happening?"

"Bridget can't remember the name of her window washer," reported Bessie.

"Oh, wow!" commented Hope.

"Bridget is on a panel and has to give a talk," added Ruth.

"I know. I'm coming to hear you. It's this Wednesday, isn't it? Not the end of the world?" Hope finished on a questioning note.

"You know that," Bridget said. "And I know that, but you tell me why my blood pressure is way up, heart thumping, my sleep lousy with nightmares."

"That's unlike you," Farah said. "We rely on you to make us see our discomforts, even our disasters, as interesting experiences."

"Well, there is nothing interesting, I promise you, in not being at home when the window washer comes to wash your windows, or in being home when he comes to wash the windows and you haven't cleared a lifetime collection of colored glassware from the windowsills."

"Why not move everything and then he can come when he comes?"

"And live, for who knows how long, in a world with glass objects on every surface?"

Ilka said, "I must have quoted to you my old friend Carter, who numbered the things that do not matter, which drove him to drink? 'It do not matter' became our watchword. It's surprising how many things that applies to."

Bridget said, "Anxiety is surprisingly uncomfortable. I remember and long for my normal, well-enough-regulated self. It's like not being able to imagine summer afternoons when your coat won't zip on a windy street corner in February."

"Wait! Hang on," Hope said. "Now imagine Hell as an eternal February on a windy corner with the zipper irreparably broken."

"What sin is it punishment for?" Ruth asked.

"No sin. Pure punishment. The greatest imaginable discomfort without the possibility of change or end is my idea of Hell. What's yours?"

"I've got a good one," Farah said. "Being on a telephone hold that cannot be disconnected and will never be answered."

They took turns imagining eternities of what each thought unbearable until Bessie said, "Watching my Colin in pain."

Here's where Hope opened the bottle of wine she had brought, and Bridget said, "My anxiety is a moderate Hell, like a low-grade, generalized fear about personal stuff I don't know how to fix and the stuff in the news that nobody knows how to fix, so I'm going to do what I know how to do, which is to write a story and call it 'Funk.'"

Death of the Water Bug

LUCINELLA WROTE TO BRIDGET: 'We never outlive a shy, uncomfortable shame before asking a friend, especially another writer, to give us the time and attention to read what we have written. *Death of the Water Bug* was accepted by a journal, had me write my 'no more than fifty-word bio' but never explained why they did not publish the story. Please, please believe that I am asking for your shamelessly honest opinion.'

Bridget replied, 'I do. I completely believe that we believe that we want our reader's honest opinion, but you and I both know that there's not one of us who does not conceal from herself the hope, the expectation, that the honest opinion will be that we have written a masterpiece.

Incidentally, I hate bugs.

Lucinella's Story

I called Eddy, our handyman, and he came up, got rid of the water bug and closed the hole behind the stove by which, he thought, the creature must have got into my kitchen.

One Week Later, as they say in the movies, Bessie was in town and came over and went to get herself a glass of water. Her scream would, in an audition for a Miss Marple episode, have landed her the character who trips over the corpse. Another water bug! Bessie grabbed her handbag and was out the front door.

"Oh come on! Come back." I had followed her into the hallway. "Bessie! I'll get rid of him! Come back inside and have a drink."

"I *hate* it!" Bessie said, visibly shuddering, and escaped into the elevator.

Getting rid of the water bug turned out not to be so simple. The animal sat on the kitchen floor. I couldn't keep calling Eddy, so I prepared myself for that crunching sound, raised my right leg and brought my shoe down where the bug was no longer sitting.

It put me in mind of a Robert Frost poem in which the poet's pencil point fails to eliminate the spot on the paper before him because the spot has run away and continues running with such frantic intentionality, the poet comments that it's not on every page one has the good fortune to meet with such an active intelligence.

The water bug had chosen not to be stepped on. His abhorrence of being dead gave his six legs a surely admirable burst of speed into the black region under the sink where he knew – yes, the animal knew that I was not able to get at him.

THE NEXT TIME BESSIE WAS IN TOWN, I invited her to watch the exquisite French film called *Microcosmos* which says that it is about "the people of the grass."

"Bugs!" Bessie said, but she sat down and we watched two lady bugs on a stalk that bends under their combined weight while they share a drink from opposite sides of the same dew drop.

"Lady bugs are okay," Bessie said.

"My favorite is the dung beetle," I said.

"HATE it!" Bessie said and reached for her handbag.

I said, "Bessie, watch!"

The beetle is transporting its ball of dung from somewhere to somewhere else by walking on its front legs, using the superior strength of the two back legs with the assistance of the middle pair to do the pushing. I don't know if it's because it is walking backwards, or because of all that nervous urgency, it takes the animal a moment to know that the dungball has got hoisted onto the point of an up-standing little twig. Now what? What, if it is not the operation of thinking, stops the beetle from pushing at the side, which is not working and starts it pushing from the bottom up to dislodge the dung from what it was stuck on?

"Yuck!" Bessie said.

"Watch!" I said. Here's where the camera backs away and up to a height that gives an overview of the terrain across which the animal needs (oh, reason not the need) to transport its dung it alone knows where. Bessie got up.

"Bessie, stay, please. Sit. I want to argue. "

Bessie sat reluctantly down.

"Why is it," I asked her, "that you, a five-foot nine-inch human cannot – and I totally believe that you can really not be in a room – would rather not be in the same apartment as an animal that stands less than an inch off the ground, who runs away and hides under the sink because he has no apparatus with which to do you the least harm?"

Bessie said, "Imagine that bug walking over your bed, no! crawling up the leg of your pants…"

"It's true," I said, "that I can't think of the water bug as a she. But have you seen him rub his head between his two antennae? Don't you love the housefly when it does that thing like washing its hands?"

Bessie said that she did not care to think about bugs doing cute people-things. "Insects," she said, "are the non-human, the not-us. Insects are our Other."

"The other," I said, "whom we are meant to learn, if not to like, to at least love, because they perfectly resemble us, in not wanting to be stepped on, not to be squashed underfoot, who want so immensely to not be dead."

Bessie said, "When God decreed enmity between the human and the snake he included the creepy crawlies with their six legs, their sectioned bodies that have the plumbing on the outside, and no fur or feather with which to cover themselves."

I said, "Okay! If we're playing Bible, I see your Genesis and raise you a Pharaoh. 'Swarming!' is the verb for the infestation of Hebrews in Goshen."

"So where are you going with this?"

"Isn't it interesting that both Pharaoh and Hitler wanted to be rid of us and that both put every roadblock in our way to stop us from leaving?"

Bessie continued in the expressive pose of one waiting for further explanation or enlightenment.

"Well anyway," I argued, "Jaques says that we are the usurpers, who 'fright the animals and kill them up in their assigned and native dwelling place.'"

"In the Forest of Arden!" cried Bessie. "You're not going to claim that the house-fly, the pantry moth, and the cockroach have rights in the New York kitchen?"

"From their viewpoint, they have. In my student days, I shared my room with a little velvet mouse. In the stillness of midnight it made a surprising racket inside the waste paper basket and left little poops behind my illicit hotplate. When I put the light on it was sitting between two broken parquet tiles. It pointed its little face this way, that way, this way."

"And what will you do when you have your next infestation of cockroaches?" Bessie asked me.

"Call Eddy," I said, "and Eddy will call the exterminator."

Bessie said she HATED cockroaches, got her handbag and left, left me wondering if it isn't morally cleaner to do good to your friends and harm your enemies, and if that included the animals who merely annoy or disgust us.

THE WATER BUG IS BACK. How many days has it been? No running now. I watch him slouch out from behind the sink, his head low to the ground, limping sideways as if his feet hurt. In the end of Kafka's story, the housemaid's broom sweeps the dead bug out the kitchen door. Nothing easier than for me to bring my shoe down on a senescent water bug. I wipe up his remains with the corner of a paper towel and drop it in the garbage, a minor sample of the world's sadness.

BRIDGET WROTE LUCINELLA, "Wonderful that our idea is never new under the sun. Shakespeare said it in a single sentence: *And the poor beetle, that we tread upon / In corporal sufferance finds a pang as great / As when a giant dies.*"

Left Shoulders

ILKA SAID, "You remember how we said 'No more planes, no more trains'?"

"And no more movies," added Farah. "No more going to the theatre."

"Or going anywhere. Going out," Bessie said. "Eve asks me don't I want to take a turn down on Riverside Drive, and I say no. I want to sit where I am sitting."

"There have been times, lately," Ilka said, "when I've thought, No more talking. There's something I want to say, but my mouth doesn't open to say it, or not in the moment when there is a gap in the conversation. I remember my mother sitting beside me at our dinner parties – it was she who had usually cooked. Was I aware, in the heat of what I was saying to whoever sat on my right, of her sitting behind my left shoulder? Did I understand that she no longer had what it takes to make her way into the conversation?"

"The energy to self-start," Hope said, "to insert oneself."

Ilka said, "I would go on and on, talking and talking."

"So many left shoulders," Bessie said.

"I used to have an Indian friend, Padma," said Ilka. "Padma might be sitting on the sofa talking with me, and if my husband walked in she would minimally adjust herself to also face him, and if my mother came in, Padma, with the most natural, littlest movement, turned to include her also. It was the prettiest thing to observe. We in the West seem not to have that instinct or that skill. My friend John comes to see me and we are talking. The bell rings and it's my friend Joe. In another minute, John and Joe are talking and I am behind their two left shoulders."

Bessie said, "Old people seem always, at any table, to be sitting on the wrong side of left shoulders."

Hope said, "Lotte used to make us laugh at her old-people stories where old meant being forty or thirty, she sitting in the passenger seat and the driver not flirting with her."

Bridget said, "Nobody ever flirted with me. I don't think I knew how. But I used to congratulate myself that, having been a plain girl, I had become a rather well-looking old person. Then I read Proust's description of the party where he almost mistakes his first love for her mother. She has grown old, all his friends are old. He, Marcel, is old. I was amused that it hurt my feelings when he says that the woman who smiles at him is old and ugly."

"But we have the blessed Zoom," Bessie said, "where we are small and at a distance. Zoom hides more than our wrinkles. Much to be said for Zoom."

"But I was surprised," Bridget said, "that it hurt my feelings when he said old and ugly."

Why with an Exclamation

AT ONE OLD ROCKINGHAM LUNCH before Colin's illness – so it must have been some three or more years ago, Bridget thought – Colin had invited everyone out on his boat. Bessie had stayed in to deal with the complications of lunch. Hope and Farah opted to help her, but Bridget and Ruth went sailing with Colin. Ruth soon wanted to get back to firm land, but for Bridget it was bliss, the revelation of what she felt she had been born to do, to be.

Today, they were seated at Bridget's table. Handing around plates and passing the salad, she was reluctant to say what was going to take too long and be too cumbersome. The friends were all readers, but she alone kept returning to Proust. Still, she set sail. "The payoff," she said, "is that you come across improbable behaviors and recognize your friends – recognize yourself."

"Like what, for instance?" her friends obliged her by asking.

Bridget said, "Marcel's father has been more than hinting – has been nudging his excellent friend, whose name I'm not even going to try to recall, for membership in the Institute, to which the friend has the means to get him elected. Well, why does the friend not act for him?

"So Proust tells another story," continued Bridget, feeling that she was getting farther and farther from the home shore. "Marcel's father invites a family friend to dinner. Knowing dear old Swann's desire to meet a certain young woman, he does not invite the young woman."

"And how does that explain anything?" asked Hope.

"It illustrates the ancient truth that 'To those who have, shall be given; from those who have not, shall be taken even that they have,'" Bridget explained. "But Proust is saying that the trick of generally well-constituted natures is to not give a friend what the friend wants."

"But why do we?" Bessie said. "That doesn't explain why we do that."

Bridget said, "This is not the 'why' that expects a 'because.' It's the 'Why, how curious,' with an exclamation mark!"

Next to Godliness

AT MONDAY'S LADIES' LUNCH, Bridget told her friends the bad thing she had done on her way over. "My neighbor from 6-J got on the elevator and asked me how I was doing, and, instead of saying 'Fine,' I said, 'I've had the worst morning! I'm bringing my friends a bottle of wine and went to open the cupboard for a bag and out fell an avalanche of who knows how many years' worth of paper bags that I must have kept, for whatever future use or need I may have imagined, stuffed in anyhow just anywhere.'"

The shifting and resettling on chairs might have alerted Bridget that she was wearying her friends' interest and attention. Not knowing where she was headed, she continued, "Why, when I already had my coat on, did I start to organize the large and the midsize into separate piles, the small throwaways without handles on the left, and those handsomely engineered to be refolded on the right?"

Lucinella said, "There was a time when I needed, when I had to have my pencils in a row, sharpened to perfect points, all of one length, which, of course, they couldn't remain unless I kept getting rid of the wrong size."

"My friend Dario," Ruth said, "used to come in and sit and talk and fidget and look uncomfortable until he suddenly got up and straightened the picture on the opposite wall."

Hope said, "The nice woman who comes in once a week to clean doesn't put things back where they belong."

"Tell her you want the right things in the right place," Bessie said.

"Oh, I tell her. I tell her and tell her and tell her. I think she may really not remember where things are supposed to go."

"Does it matter?" Ilka asked her.

"It so obviously doesn't, so why is it driving me insane?"

Bessie said, "My Eve and Jenny are terminally untidy, which reminds me of my mother standing in my doorway saying it looked as if a band of robbers had gone through the things in my room."

The group considered Bessie to be the arbiter of Ladies' Lunch agendas. This week she had e-mailed them an idea suggested by a recent *New York Times* article that, she explained, "compared our children's relations with us with our attitudes toward the adults of our day."

"And *my* suggestion," put in Ruth, "was that we should think about what our lot understands by 'wokeness.'"

Lucinella said, "I don't know that I know what exactly it is."

"That's what I want us to talk about."

"Yes," Bridget said, "yes, but *why* do Hope's things need to be in the right place?"

"So she can find them?" suggested Farah.

"I grant you that, O.K.," Bridget said. "But that is not why we arrange things in rows. Who benefits from my smoothing the wrinkles of my bedcover? Why do I correct what is off-center?"

"Because you want things to look neat and tidy."

"I do. I know I do. But *why* do I? What's it for? Why do we neaten nature into gardens? What is the virtue of a tidy grass border? And why did I take the trouble to hang the picture parallel to the floor in the first place?"

"Well, jeez, you wouldn't purposely hang it askew."

"No. I certainly would not," said Bridget. "That's what I *mean*. Why not?"

Bessie said, "Do you remember Lotte saying that things not put properly away were like 'visual noise'? Don't we have a need – don't we yearn for order?"

There followed a moment in which Bridget did not say "*Why* do we?," Bessie was remembering where Lotte used to sit, with her back to the window, and Farah understood that she was seeing her friends across the table as if through a plastic baggie.

Ruth picked up the *Times* and put it down again: they were not going to talk about wokeness.

Hope said, "Isn't 'neatliness' supposed to be next to 'godliness'?"

Bessie said, "That order is better than disorder is self-explanatory. "

"Explain it," said Bridget.

Beyond Imagining

BESSIE, LOTTE, RUTH, FARAH, AND BRIDGET had agreed without the need for discussion that they were not going to pass, pass away, and under no circumstances on. They were going to die. It was now several years since Lotte had died in an assisted-living facility. Then, when Covid worried their children, Ruth had undertaken to Zoom Ladies' Lunch. She suggested that anyone who had something to say should show a hand.

Farah put up her hand. She said, "I don't find it difficult to think about...," then paused in surprise at not being able to say "dying," "about choosing not to live if I'm going blind."

Bessie, Zooming from Old Rockingham, said, "That would be Colin's choice when he hurts and he hurts all the time."

Bridget raised her hand. "I think that the reason I think I won't mind being dead is that I can't imagine it, and I don't think we know how to believe what we aren't able to imagine."

"You want to repeat that?" Ruth asked her.

"No," Bridget said and laughed. "I'm not sure that I could."

THEN COLIN DIED and Bessie allowed herself to collapse. Her daughter Eve called Ruth to tell her that Bessie was in a Connecticut hospital. Ruth called her there and reported to the group: "Bessie says the room is bright and pleasant enough. I lamely asked her how she was feeling, and she said, 'Sad. Sad and ill.'"

When Farah called her, Bessie said, "Eve wants me to temporarily move into our minuscule Ninety-fourth Street pied-à-terre, which I had made over to her."

"That's a good plan, is it, temporarily?"

"Temporarily. Colin and I agreed that Old Rockingham must go to his children. It was never my world. There's a line I remember, from I forget which school poem, to 'dance an hour beneath the beeches.' That's what my Connecticut years have been. It's New York that's for real."

HOPE SAID, "Ruth has been hosting our Zooms all this time and we've never done her agenda."

Ruth asked, "What's my agenda? I forget."

"You said you wanted us to discuss our take on wokeness?"

"Which is not a word in the Oxford English Dictionary," said Ilka, and Bridget said, "Use 'wokeness' in a sentence."

"Just vote it in the next election," Ruth said.

Farah took out her phone and read: " 'Wokeness. The quality of being alert to and concerned about social injustice and discrimination.' "

"What we used to call being a liberal," said Ilka.

"With the gloves off," said Ruth.

"I'm trying to remember who described liberals as not having enough sense to argue in favor of their own opinions," Ilka said.

"That's nice. I like that," said Bridget, brightening. "I'm going to write a story about two liberals fighting a duel. On the count of ten, they turn and each shoots himself in the foot."

"Herself in the foot," Ruth said.

"Themself," said Ilka.

RUTH CALLED FARAH and said, "I've been feeling stupid and woozy. The doctor is doing tests."

Farah said, "Can I come and visit you? How is Monday?"

"Monday is good," Ruth said.

Ruth's elegant daughter opened the door. "It's Helena, isn't it?" Farah said, remembering her from a long-ago mother-and-daughter Ladies' Lunch.

Helena said, "Mom is expecting you. Mom, it's Farah."

Ruth in a severely buttoned dress and slippers was sitting in an ample wing chair in the familiar living room. Her son, Ben, introduced himself and asked if it was too early for a glass of wine. Ruth said, "The doctor says it will do no harm."

"Then yes, please," Farah said, and Ben left the room.

Ruth said, "I have a tumor."

"Do we know what that means?" asked Farah.

Ruth said, "I find I'm grateful for that conversation," and Farah understood her to mean the conversation about dying and said, "I've been trying to think that I've had the use of my eyes for upward of ninety years and it doesn't seem unreasonable to be expected to give them up." She paused and said, "One looks for a way to think about it."

Ruth said, "They may try radiation, but the doctor says it will do no good."

The son returned with two small glasses of wine. There were the minutes occupied by the business of clearing two surfaces where the two glasses could stand within easy reach. Ben left the room. Farah was aware of searching for something to talk about. She talked about Bessie temporarily sharing the Ninety-fourth Street pied-à-terre with her daughter Eve.

Ruth said, "Temporarily?"

"Colin has left Old Rockingham to his children."

Farah told Ruth about Ilka's latest argument with her cousin Frieda; she talked about Trump, about Bibi and Jerusalem. She said, "Is next Monday good to come and see you? Bridget wants to come."

"Next Monday is good," Ruth said.

IT IS THE NURSE who brings Farah and Bridget into the empty living room, goes out and returns with Ruth in a wheelchair. The nurse goes out. Ruth looks like Ruth but her voice is so low that they have to ask her to repeat what she is saying: "My right side has shut down. I don't have the use of my hand." The nurse comes back with three small glasses of wine, for which she arranges three convenient surfaces. The nurse goes out.

Ruth watches Farah and Bridget talk.

WHEN, THE FOLLOWING MONDAY, Ilka and Hope ring the doorbell, Helena opens the door and says, "Mom is unresponsive, but come in." Ruth is sitting in the wheelchair. They sit down. No wine, thank you. Helena remains in the room. The fingers of Ruth's left hand play a nonexistent keyboard on her lap. She looks into the room before her but does not speak.

Afterward, Ilka and Hope talk over a cup of coffee in the corner Starbucks. Hope says, "One yearns to be comfortable for her, but one just sits there."

Ilka says, "I looked up 'tumor' and it's too much information. What does it mean that 'the body shuts down'?"

Hope says, "What is the Ruth in the wheelchair thinking? What do we know? Is she in pain?"

BESSIE COMES TO SEE RUTH and takes her hand and presses it to her cheek, weeps and says, "Colin is dead."

Ruth frowns – is it in an attempt to focus? She says, "Who?"

AND ANOTHER MONDAY. Helena says, "There's a theory that hearing is the last faculty to go. We asked Mom whether she wanted music, and she said, 'Conversation.'"

Helena, Farah, Bridget, and Ilka make conversation. Ruth, in a blue bathrobe and slippers, lies on the sofa. Her head is turned away from the room and the people in it. The open window behind her gives onto a magnificent view of the Hudson River. The fingers of Ruth's left hand move on her lap. She coughs – is it to clear an obstruction in her throat?

Farah

THE SEASON AFTER RUTH DIED and Covid was over as much as it was ever going to be, the friends talked about reviving Ladies' Lunches in person. "At my place, please, if you don't mind," Farah said. "My new walker gets me around the apartment, but I no longer feel secure on the street."

Bessie, about to close up the Connecticut house, did not feel like a trip to town, so Farah set up the computer on the lunch table and Bessie Zoomed in to what turned out to be "a bit of a downer," as Hope put it. What was wrong with each of them could not be contained within the twenty minutes allotted to complaining: since Colin's death, Bessie suffered from debilitating headaches; Hope was scheduled for a pacemaker; Bridget might need meniscus surgery;

and Lucinella's "Book of Late Verses" had not been reviewed by the *Times*. Ilka detailed the dental repair she accused herself of neglecting.

"And I," Farah said, "can no longer see to read the pages of instructions my ophthalmologist sends home with me."

"But you're a doctor," Hope said. "Doesn't that give you insights?"

Farah said, "I always liked the bit in *Washington Square* where the father of – what's the girl's name? – gets ill. He's a doctor and he instructs the household what to do and when. What I understand is that there are a lot of different things going wrong with my eyes."

"Like what?" Bridget asked her.

"There is an interestingly patterned white lace across my field of vision, sometimes a field of white or purple daisies with yellow centers, in gentle, continual right-to-left motion, without moving."

"What is motion without moving? Sounds like T. S. Eliot," Lucinella said.

Farah said, "I hold up my hand and watch the lace or the daisies – I'm just describing what I see –

moving without ever disappearing in the direction in which they are moving. What do I know? I ask the doctor and he says many people report that the loss of vision finds compensation in visual hallucinations. Which explains exactly nothing."

"How many fingers?" Ilka asked her.

"That's not the problem," said Farah. "Let me give you the plastic-baggie test. I carry one with me in my pocket for the purpose. Look through this and count my fingers."

"Four fingers," Ilka said. "I see your four fingers. I see you. I see the room but everything is behind a dark, a dirty mist."

Farah said, "And I ask the doctor how thick and how much darker will the mist get? How dark? Will there be an absence of light, a black darkness? How black is black? Is it too cold for ice cream?" she asked the friends around the table. "Berries and ice cream, everybody? Anybody?"

Before the next lunch, Farah e-mails UWSLadies Lunch. Subject line: "Black Is Black."

Interesting. Last night I had finished cleaning up my supper dishes. You all know my kitchen, Upper West Side, sausage-shaped. It is too narrow for my walker, which was O.K. because I was able to reach things on both sides and touch either wall on my way to the door, where I turned off the light and then reached around the darkness outside for my walker.

Which was not where I thought I had left it. When I turned around to put the kitchen light back on, I couldn't find the switch, couldn't find where the entrance to the kitchen might be. I had been a good citizen and turned off all the lights on my way to the kitchen so that now I was moving in total darkness and I did not recognize the objects that met my hands - the doorknob of a door I could not identify. I touched books, a shelf? There is no bookshelf near the kitchen door. Completely disoriented, I could not tell where in my apartment I had got to, where there was another door with a wall on the left...

I don't know how long I stumbled around hoping for something – something that I knew – to grab onto, before I saw the city lights of Lower Manhattan in the uncurtained window in my bedroom and turned on the bedside light.

My trial run?

I ask the doctor if I will go blind and he doesn't say – would rather not say? Or is it that we doctors don't know?

.

Bessie

"'If not now, when?'" quoted Bridget, when the friends met at Farah's apartment once again. "I would give up a lifetime's writing to have got that thought into those four words."

"No, you wouldn't," Ilka said. "You wouldn't give up writing."

"And that's true, too," Bridget said. "I don't know what to do with myself between my morning coffee and lunch at noon if I'm not writing something, and I wish one of you would have a complaint or a disaster for me to write about."

"Have some sushi," said Farah.

Bessie said, "Write about our neighbor Bains buying Old Rockingham, going to change the locks a week from Monday. Eve and Jenny drove me up and we had the week to get rid of the things there's no room for in Eve's studio. And what if my next move might be to assisted living?"

Bessie's friends were silent and looked at her. "My clothes and my own stuff were not the problem," Bessie continued. "Eve had packed me up when I was in hospital. It's this endless accumulation of what our kids are supposed to deal with after we're dead."

The friends around the table looked at Bessie.

She said, "The local antique dealer came. He took the Bennington ware, some silver, some books and things, and left us to get rid of just so much stuff. There was Colin's mother's unfinished patchwork – "

"You're not going to throw out old patchwork!" they all said.

"And the ancient kitchen scales," Bessie said. "The cookware, cookbooks, more cookbooks, three inkwells, a box of fountain pens. Jenny made a pile of the useless things for garbage pickup and Eve went out and brought back what she thought was well designed or beautiful."

"I know, oh, I know!" Hope said. "I'm a lifelong collector of postcards and clippings from magazines."

"Clippings? Clippings of what?"

"Anything I thought beautiful. Art. What interested, excited, irritated, puzzled me. There's a suitcase of my favorites under the bed, and the box of favorite favorites in the foyer. In more than a decade, there has been no moment when I have taken them out and looked at them. There's a drawer full of these snippets in the closet that I am going to have to empty for Miranda. My granddaughter is moving in with me."

"Moving in! Goodness! I mean, is that good?" Farah asked her.

"Delightful," Hope said, "except that carving out room for Miranda is a complication; I have stopped sleeping. Yesterday, I got the wastepaper basket, put that drawer on the table, and picked out one snippet after another snippet after another and put one after another back in the drawer and put the drawer back in the closet."

"You didn't throw any of them away!" Ilka said.

"Two," Hope said. "Write, Bridget, about the things we don't need, don't know what to do with but cannot throw away. It feels like a physical inability to let things go."

"Like the key," Bessie said, "from when we were leaving Old Rockingham. We'd done the upstairs and cased the downstairs for anything we'd forgotten. Jenny was already in the driver's seat, Eve put the last bag into the trunk, and I closed the door of the house. Jenny said, 'Mom, just leave the key. Bains is coming over to change the lock.' I said, 'I know, but I'd better hold on to it.' Eve said, 'Mom! What on earth for?'

"I said, 'Just in case.'

" 'In case of what?' they asked me.

"I said I didn't know."

In the Mail

Once [writers have] finished a new manuscript and put it in the mail, they exist in a state of suspended emotional and psychic animation... and it's cruelty to animals to keep them waiting.

ROBERT GOTTLIEB, THE PARIS REVIEW

"LET'S GET THE COMPLAINING out of the way," proposed Hope. "I've got me a pacemaker."

Farah said, "I'm losing my vision."

Bessie said, "I lost my husband."

And Bridget said, "I sent my story to a friend from my old writing class."

"And how is that a complaint?" Bessie asked her.

Bridget said, "Because it feels – maybe it's something like the actor's stage fright."

"What I felt," Lucinella said to Bridget, "when I sent you my water-bug story. Embarrassed."

"Water bugs! Yuck!" everybody said, and Bessie said, "But why is it embarrassing?"

Bridget said, "There's a kind of shyness or shame to be demanding another person's time and attention."

"Of exposing oneself," Lucinella said. "I begged Bridget for her honest opinion, and Bridget wrote me that there is not one of us who doesn't conceal from herself the hope, the expectation, that the honest opinion will be that we have written a masterpiece."

"And the fear," Bridget added, "that we will be found out to be a jackass."

"What's your story about?" Farah asked Bridget.

"About a group of women friends getting old together."

"About us, you mean," Hope said.

"About us, but you understand that I write stories. About us sitting round the table and talking, but not necessarily what we say and not identifiably any one of us."

"But why not identifiably us?" asked Farah.

"Maybe so as not to make public what we feel free to tell each other in private; to not offend with what I understand or misunderstand. And because I've already killed off two of us on the page. But really it's about how we make up the people in our stories."

"Only we're right here. You don't have to make us up."

"Yes, I do. I don't have to invent, but I have to imagine us. People, pacemakers, and glaucoma are not the stuff that can be pasted into a Microsoft document or onto a sheet of paper. Remember *Star Trek*? You're beamed to a different dimension by being decimated and then reassembled on arrival. I turn us into the words that would allow my friend Anna to imagine us."

"So what did your Anna think of us?"

"She didn't."

"How do you mean?"

"I haven't heard from her."

"When did you send her your story?"

"Tomorrow will be four weeks to the day."

"So what will you do?"

"Lie in bed at night and stew. Dream vengeful dreams. Or imagine Anna putting off the obligation to read my story. I picture her putting off the reading in order to put off the barely thinkable prospect of having to say something to me if she doesn't like it or doesn't get the point, and so she puts it off and puts it off until she forgets about it and, eventually, forgets the cause of the pinpoint of guilt in the lower left back side of her brain."

"Poor Anna," said everybody.

Grandmother Mole

HOPE SAID, "MY AGENDA? Falling asleep at the movies."

Farah said, "Now that it's hard for me to read, I lie on my bed and listen to YouTube philosophy which I don't understand."

"What don't you understand?" Bridget asked her. They were talking on Zoom.

"What is 'the excluded middle'?" Farah said. "And how does the inability of the finite to imagine the infinite prove the existence of God?"

Bridget said, "I've been reading *The Peaceable Kingdom* with great-granddaughter Libby. 'The lion shall lie down with the lamb and little Libby will lead them.'"

Bessie said, "Lucky you to still have a little Libby to read to. My Eve's Johnny used to like it when I read him the story of Mole who shouts and shouts and doesn't stop shouting until his Grandmother Mole figures out that what he means is 'Notice me.'"

"Yesterday," continued Bessie, "I was coming out of the building, when who should be walking up the street but Johnny. 'You are coming to see me!' I said. Why, he said - wasn't I feeling well? I was O.K., I told him. He told me that he was on his way up the block to study with his friend in his friend's new place, and he said goodbye and I said goodbye. Is it unreasonable of me to think he might have some feelings for his grandmother now that I have lost Colin?"

"Colin wasn't his real grandfather," Hope said.

"Maybe not, but he was just lovely with the boy. Used to take him sailing, with me, terrified, watching from the deck of the house."

"When they turn teens," Farah said, "we know it isn't grandmothers they have on their souls. If I live long enough, Hami will become a grown-up and we may be friends again."

Ilka said, "Not necessarily. Maggie is looking through my papers and found – wait!" Ilka disappeared from the screen and returned holding up a fragile postcard. "It's dated 1889, from the grandmother I never knew to my father. A loose translation: 'My dearest, so very beloved Hansl, How is it possible that you have not in a whole week found the smallest little minute to send one line to your mama...'"

"The ur-complaint. Right out of Nichols and May," said Lucinella. "Listen!" She manipulated her iPad.

A woman's voice said, "This is your mother. Do you remember me?"

A male voice said, "I was just going to call you... Do you know that I had my finger on the – "

The mother said, "I sat by that phone all day Friday, and all Friday night, all day Saturday, and all day Sunday. Finally, your father said to me, Phyllis, eat something, you'll faint. I said, Harold, no, I don't want to have my mouth full when my son calls me..."

The son's voice: "I feel awful." The mother: "Oh, honey, if I could believe that, I'd be the happiest mother in the world."

AT THE FOLLOWING LADIES' LUNCH, Bridget read the friends the Nichols-and-May Mole story she had written.

She read: "When Grandmother Mole met Mole outside her tunnel, she said, 'I've been waiting for you.' 'Why, Grandmother Mole, aren't you feeling well?' Mole asked her, but Grandmother Mole was feeling well enough. She said, 'It's just I want to see you.' 'Grandmother Mole, do you need me to go hunting for you?' 'No, thank you,' Grandmother Mole said.'"

Bridget interrupted her story to say, "I was going to check Wikipedia. What do moles hunt? Do moles hunt? So, anyway. 'Grandmother Mole,' Mole asked her, 'do you need me to come and dig you a new tunnel?' But there was nothing wrong with Grandmother Mole's old tunnel. 'What I want,' Grandmother Mole said to her Mole, 'is for you to want to visit me, to want to talk and to be with me.'"

"She means 'Notice me,'" commented Farah.

Bridget returned to her story. "'So goodbye, Grandmother Mole,' Mole said. And he walked up the block to his friend's tunnel to study."

"To hang out," amended Farah.

Bessie said, "Oh, leave him be. Let him hang out or study or do whatever kids do."

"What has happened to you?" Lucinella asked Bessie. "What has changed?"

Bessie said, "My grandson e-mailed me. I thought all the kids ever did was 'text' each other."

She pulled out a piece of paper. "Johnny wrote me: 'I'm sorry I haven't been available recently!!! How are you? Let's have lunch or dinner soon. I miss you.'"

Ilka

"TODAY," ILKA SAID, "my Maggie is finally getting her Austrian citizenship."

"Congratulations!" "Great!" "That's wonderful!" said the Zoom gallery of friends. They were back on their computers.

"I guess," Ilka said. "It seemed to take years of consultations with consulates, documentations. Her birth certificate had to be certified, et cetera, et cetera, a lot of et ceteras."

"You didn't apply for citizenship for yourself?"

Ilka said, "I did not. I was remembering my parents' desperation assembling the papers that were required for our emigration – the morning post that didn't bring the essential documents before the expiration of two other essential documents.

"Austria had annulled our citizenship. It bemused me to have been not only stateless but unnatural until I became a naturalized American."

"But that's not what the word means," Bridget said. "It means a plant growing naturally where it's not indigenous."

Ilka said, "Maggie has bought her ticket to Vienna, where I was indigenous."

"And you're not going?"

Ilka said, "You remember how we said no more trains, no more planes?"

"But you've been back?"

"I used to go."

"And how was that?"

"Intensely exciting – the child-in-the-candy-store kind of exciting. I would deposit my bags in the hotel and shoot back out the door in search of a certain palace I remembered on the other side of the street, or a tower glimpsed in the other direction, but I'd get waylaid by an archway and stop to look into a shadowy courtyard with an old water cistern. I remember looking through one open door at a monumental Baroque male supporting the central staircase on his bare back.

"The Viennese dialect of my childhood sounded helplessly dear. The taxi driver from the airport told me I was lucky that I had got away before the Russians came. My hosts were kind and eager, the children, or grandchildren, surely, of erstwhile anti-Nazis, but by the third day I wanted to be out of there and was glad to find my seat on the plane taking me back to my adoptive New York."

"That had naturalized you," Bridget said.

ILKA SAID, "You've all seen our family portrait. Let me go get it and I'll show you. Maggie spent the weekend with me."

She held it up in front of the monitor. "You see how the photographer has staged the fifteen children – fourteen, actually, because Karl, the youngest, was not born yet – around the father standing behind the seated mother. The three oldest girls are Great Aunt Berta's, this is the one I call Mali, and Rosa. I've told you about the Sunday afternoons we used to spend in Tante Mali's apartment with my mother's cousins."

Farah said, "The aunt who had a stereopticon?"

"Who let you mess with the beads on her curtains," remembered Bessie.

Ilka said, "The little Onkel Löwy would open the front door into the foyer and show us into the room where Tante Mali with the lovely face, immensely overweight, always sat in the same chair at the big table watching us. You see, in the picture, she is the one with the sweet look. She and Onkel Löwy ended up in Mauthausen.

"Sitting on her left, that's my grandmother Rosa, around fifteen, maybe. She and the four-year-old Poldi on the low stool would make it out and get to New York. They and the brother who went to Canada before the First World War, and a brother who died of lung disease, were the four 'survivors' of my grandmother's generation.

"All the boys in the picture – what age would you say, between seven and seventeen? – have had their heads shaved for the photograph and wear big bow ties. No way for me to tell Maggie which one grew up to be Gigerl, who got away to Canada, or Miklosz, who had the bookshop, or Szandor, married to Tante Mali, who had twins, one of whom, Willi, lives in Israel. Which and what was the name of the uncle who had a photo shop with a Bauhaus-style interior?"

"Maggie is in Vienna, in Wien," Ilka told her friends on their next Zoom. "She has taken the best I can do in the way of a family tree – the old, broken leather address book – and seems to know how to do the research I didn't do. Was it Rotenturm or Sterngasse where my parents lived after I left? My grandparents moved in with them after the Nazis Aryanized Grandfather's house and shop.

"Maggie e-mails that it was Rotenstern Strasse. She e-mails me the street names of my childhood – Albert Gasse, where I went to school. The bookshop was in the Wollzeile. She has sent a picture of a block of flats. Do I recognize No. 8 Holland Strasse, Tante Mali's address? I don't. I remember the stereopticon, the tall blue tile stove in the corner, the drapes with the wooden beads, the smiling Tante Mali who sat and watched us."

"A NOTE FROM MAGGIE," says Ilka. "Maggie has visited the Wiesenthal Institute, which keeps the records. Not Mauthausen, as I said. 'On September 24, 1942, Amalie and Maximilian Löwy were deported to Theresienstadt. Deported to Auschwitz, May 16, 1944, where they perished.'

"Where they perished," Ilka says and is silent.

She imagines the days, the week expecting the knock, the banging on the front door. Two uniforms stand outside, walk through the door, they are inside the foyer – the men Hannah Arendt means, doing a job? They transport the old couple to where men will sport with them before they kill them. Ilka tries not to imagine Tante Mali, who needs help getting up from her chair, forced to run to the right, turn and run left. To imagine the men? Not Dante, not Milton, not Shakespeare has anatomized their human hearts, and about what she cannot imagine she cannot think and I cannot write.

Who Is Outside?

LADIES' MOVIE NIGHT. The friends, who have become less and less willing to leave their homes, agree to watch a movie on the TV and then meet on Zoom to talk. But here Ilka proves, as she herself says, a dead loss. "I turned it off before the tall guy, who doesn't know, is about to walk into the room."

"But that's the payoff for all that good suspense!" Bessie says. "That's the edge-of-the-chair moment we have been waiting for."

"That's why I turned it off," Ilka says.

"You don't like suspense?"

"*Hate* it. Can't stomach suspense. I mean that my physical stomach does a number on me."

"And last week you didn't finish watching *The Quiet Place*, and that was a nice suspense, a happy ending."

Ilka says, "There are no happy endings."

"It's odd," Bessie says, "because you always seem the reasonable one of us."

"I've been having nasty nights," says Ilka.

Here is something they all understand: "You don't sleep and you have horrible dreams?"

"A revolving dream," Ilka says, "in which I must find a rhyme, like an algebra problem going around and around and around. It's this poem I'm trying to translate. Theodor Kramer was a poet in Vienna in the thirties, a Jew. My Uncle Paul's favorite writer. I've got the first verse:

Who is outside ringing at the door?
And we not even out of bed?
I'll go, love, and take a look.
Only the boy who came and left the bread.

"But the second verse:

Who is outside ringing at the door?
You stay, dear.
It was a man talking with the
neighbors asking who we are?

"When the word doesn't meet its own rhyme, we are puzzled and then we doubt," says Ilka.

Lucinella suggests, "How about 'You stay, my dear' and 'asking who we were' - a false rhyme but... "

Ilka says, "No, or maybe yes? Let it stand for the moment." She adds, "It's not the night so much as the morning hour, the hideous reëntry into the day - the day, mind you, which I rather like. I do. I like my old lady's life quite well enough. What I mean is the ugly hour before I'm awake - the necessity to wake up. Remember Lotte, the everlasting questioner, asking, 'So what is that all about?' 'Why do you? Why did you?' she would ask. And I understood that I was not so interested, that I don't much believe in my explanations.

"But may I read you the rest of the poem? And maybe you can find me a title:

Who is outside ringing at the door?
Go, love, and run the bath.
The mail has come but not the letter we were waiting
for.

Who is outside ringing at the door?
Go, my darling, turn the beds about.
It was the super.
First of next month we have to be out.

Who is outside ringing at the door?
How the fuchsia blooms so near.
Dearest, pack me my toothbrush,
and don't cry,
They are here.

PUBLICATION HISTORY

Published in The New Yorker

A Half Century Dispute (July 13, 2023).

The Forgetting Olympics; Next to Godliness; Funk; No More Trains

(*On the Agenda*, September 6, 2023).

Beyond Imagining, Farah; Bessie; Ilka

(*Beyond Imagining*, June 2, 2024).

Left Shoulders; Why with an Exclamation; Grandmother Mole

Who's Outside? (*Stories About Us*, Fall 2024).

Published in Mom Egg Review

The Death of the Water Bug (September, 2023).

Acknowledgements

Theodor Kramer's poem (p.92) is taken from his three-volume

Gesammelte Gedichte (Collected Poems), edited by Erwin Chvojka

© Paul Zsolnay Verlag, Vienna, 1997–2005.

Also by Lore Segal

Fiction

Other People's Houses (1964)
Lucinella (1976)
Her First American (1985)
An Absence of Cousins (Shakespeare's Kitchen) (2007)
Half The Kingdom (2013)
Ladies' Lunch (2023)

The Journal I Did Not Keep (ANTHOLOGY) (2019)

Translations

Gallows Songs of Christian Morgenstern (1967)
The Juniper Tree and Other Tales from Grimm (1973)
The Book of Adam to Moses (1987)
The Story of King Saul and King David (1991)

Children's Books

Tell Me a Mitzi (1970)
All the Way Home (1973)
Tell Me a Trudy (1979)
The Story of Old Mrs Brubeck and How She Looked for Trouble and Where She Found Him (1981)
The Story of Mrs Lovewright and Purrless Her Cat (1985)
Morris the Artist (2003)
Why Mole Shouted and Other Stories (2004)
More Mole Stories and Little Gopher, Too (2005)